JOHN LITHGOW

Marsupial Sue

Illustrated by

JACK E. DAVIS

Aladdin Paperbacks
New York   London   Toronto   Sydney

Marsupial Sue,

A young kangaroo,

Hated the hopping that kangaroos do.

It rattled her brain,

It gave her migraine,

A *backache*, *sideache*, *tummyache*, too.

One morning in May
Sue wandered away,
Leaving her relatives grazing on hay.

What did she see
Way up in a tree?
Koalas, gaily at play.

And suddenly Sue was convinced she had found

A way to escape all that bouncing around.

She climbed to the top,

She heard a loud POP!

And howling in pain fell again to the ground.

Marsupial Sue,

A lesson or two:

Be happy with who you are.

Don't ever stray too far from you.

Get rid of that frown

And waltz up and down

Beneath a marsupial star.

If you're a kangaroo through and through,

Just do what kangaroos do.

With summer at hand
The weather was grand,
So Sue stole away from her kangaroo band.

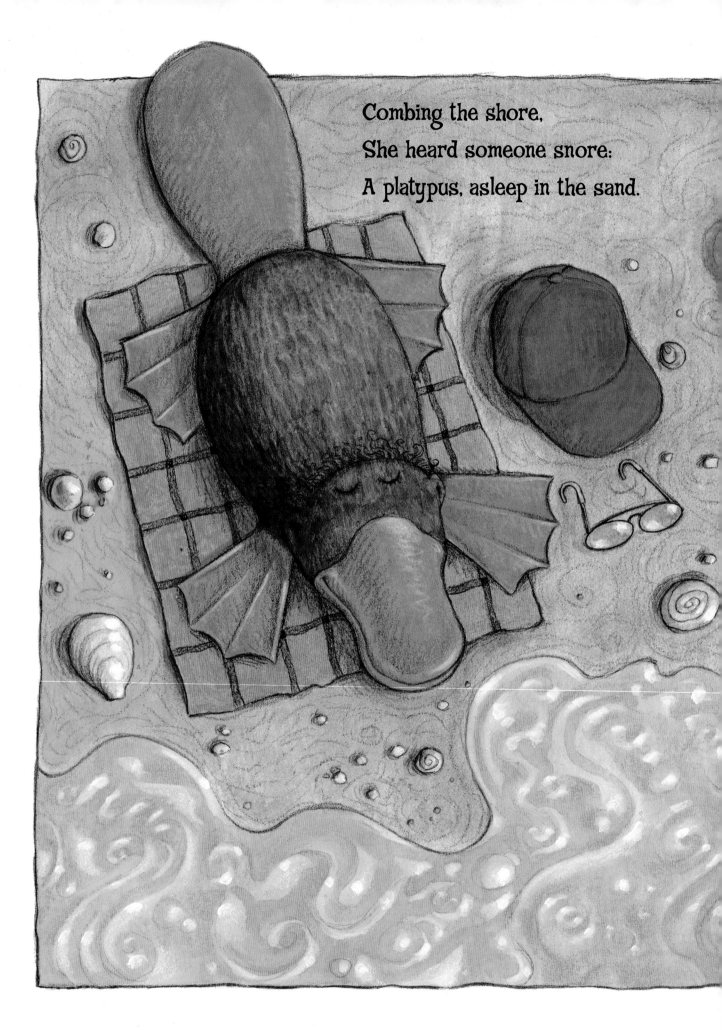

Combing the shore,
She heard someone snore:
A platypus, asleep in the sand.

"How cozy!" she said,
Completely misled,
Ignoring the probable trouble ahead,

"How perfect for me!
A life by the sea!
All snug in a watery bed!"

So she flopped in the mud with a thud and a shout.
She swallowed a scallop, a shrimp, and a trout.

By quarter to two,
The poor kangaroo
Had typhoid, pneumonia, colic, and gout.

Marsupial Sue,

A lesson or two:

Be happy with who you are.

Don't ever stray too far from you.

Get rid of that frown

And waltz up and down

Beneath a marsupial star.

If you're a kangaroo through and through,

Just do what kangaroos do.

That autumn once more

Sue got to explore

A creature she'd never laid eyes on before.

A version of her,

In miniature–

A wallaby, with cousins galore.

Before very long,
Sue joined in the throng,
Flouncing and jouncing and bouncing along.
Happy and free,
She shouted with glee:
"At last, I'm where I belong!"

Then she looked at the wallaby, sprightly and small,
Exactly like her only not quite so tall.
She widened her eyes,
And cried with surprise,
"A kangaroo's life's not so bad after all!"

Marsupial Sue,

No longer so blue:

You're happy with who you are.

You'll never stray too far from you.

You're rid of that frown,

So waltz up and down

Beneath a marsupial star.

You are a kangaroo through and through,

So do what kangaroos do.

You are a kangaroo through and through,

So do what kangaroos do.

To Sarah and Arthur, my Mom and Dad
—J. L.

For Johnny, Michael, and Baby Jason
—J. E. D.

First Aladdin Paperbacks edition September 2004

ALADDIN PAPERBACKS
An imprint of Simon & Schuster
Children's Publishing Division
1230 Avenue of the Americas
New York, NY 10020

Also available in a Simon & Schuster Books for Young Readers hardcover edition.
Designed by Paul Zakris
The text of this book was set in 18-point fink Roman.

Manufactured in China
2 4 6 8 10 9 7 5 3 1

Simon & Schuster Children's Publishing and MARSUPIAL SUE are proud
supporters of the VH1 Save The Music Foundation, a nonprofit organization that
restores music education to public schools across the country.

The Library of Congress has cataloged the hardcover edition as follows:
Lithgow, John, 1945-
Marsupial Sue / by John Lithgow ; illustrated by Jack E. Davis.
p. cm
Summary: Marsupial Sue, a young kangaroo, finds happiness in doing what kangaroos do.
ISBN 0-689-84394-1 (hc.)
[1. Kangaroos–Fiction. 2. Identity–Fiction. 3. Stories in rhyme.] I. Davis, Jack E. II. Title.
PZ8.3.L6375 Mar 2001
[E]–dc21
00-046998
ISBN 0-689-87410-3 (Aladdin pbk.)